SUGARING

by **Jessie Haas** ◆ pictures by **Jos. A. Smith**

 Greenwillow Books, New York

THANKS TO JAY BAILEY OF FAIR WINDS FARM
—J. H. AND J. A. S.

In early spring when sap rises from the roots of sugar maple trees to the buds, farmers collect some of it for making maple syrup. This does not harm the tree. All trees have sap, but only sap from sugar maples can be made into maple syrup.

Watercolor paints, colored pencils, and watercolor pencils were used for the full-color art.
The text type is Berkeley Old Style.
Text copyright © 1996 by Jessie Haas. Illustrations copyright © 1996 by Jos. A. Smith.
All rights reserved. No part of this book may be reproduced or utilized in any form
or by any means, electronic or mechanical, including photocopying, recording, or
by any information storage and retrieval system, without permission in writing from
the Publisher, Greenwillow Books, a division of William Morrow & Company, Inc.,
1350 Avenue of the Americas, New York, NY 10019.
Printed in Hong Kong by South China Printing Company (1988) Ltd.
First Edition   10   9   8   7   6   5   4   3   2   1

Library of Congress Cataloging-in-Publication Data

Haas, Jessie.
Sugaring / by Jessie Haas ; pictures by Jos. A. Smith.
        p.   cm.
Summary: Nora wants to find a way to give the horses
a special treat for helping her grandfather gather sap to
make maple syrup.
ISBN 0-688-14200-1
[1. Maple syrup—Fiction.   2. Grandfathers—Fiction.
3. Horses—Fiction.]   I. Smith, Jos. A. (Joseph Anthony),
(date) ill. II. Title.   PZ7.H1129Su   1996
95-38139   CIP   AC

FOR ROBIN ROY

—J. H.

FOR ROGER CROSSGROVE—
WHO HAS BEEN AT VARIOUS TIMES MY TEACHER,
MY LANDLORD, MY FIRST BOSS, AND ALWAYS MY GOOD FRIEND

—J. A. S.

Gramp and Nora are gathering sap. "Cold nights and sunny days—that's sugaring weather," says Gramp. Four buckets hang on one big maple tree. Gramp takes a bucket down and pours the sap into Nora's pail. When he hangs the bucket back on the tree, sap drips into it—*tap tap tap*. Gramp empties more buckets into his pails. *Tap tap TAP taptaptap* . . .

"Come up," Gramp tells the horses, and they pull the big tank closer. Their hooves sink deep in the snow. Their breath makes a cloud. Sweat rolls from under Bonnie's collar, and down Stella's nose.

"Whoa," Gramp says. He pours the sap into the tank.

One pail, two . . . Gramp waits while Nora drinks from the third pail, and he drinks too. Sap tastes good, like cold, sweet water.

"Can I give Bonnie and Stella a drink?" Nora asks. "They're working hard."

"Not from the pail," Gramp says. "They'll want to stop at every tree. I need them to stop where I say."

Nora cups her hands. She dips some sap from the pail, and she hurries to Bonnie and Stella. The sap drips out through her fingers.

Bonnie and Stella lick with their big pink tongues, but they only get a tiny taste.

"It's hard to give sap to horses," Gramp says. "Never mind—they'll get plenty of hay for lunch."

"But they get hay all the time," Nora says. "Sap is special."

When the sap is all gathered, Gramp drains
it into a holding tank.
After lunch he starts a fire in the sugar
house. Sap from the holding tank flows
into a long pan and begins to boil.
Gramp tells Nora horse stories. They feed
the fire and sing songs. Slowly the sap at
the end of the pan turns brown.

When it's almost dark out, Gramp goes to get more wood. He gives Nora a tin cup of cream. "You know what to do," he says. "I'll be right back."

Nora stands on a heavy stump, high enough to see inside the pan. She watches the brown bubbles. Are they getting higher?

All at once the bubbles lift. They almost boil over the top of the pan.

But Nora is ready. She dips her finger into the cream, and she flicks a tiny drop onto the bubbles. With a sigh they *whoosh* back down.

The horses' hooves crunch the snow. Gramp
drives them close to the sugar house.

"Whoa," he says, and hurries inside.

"It boiled up," Nora says.

"It's almost ready," Gramp says. He dips his
scoop into the pan and holds it up to watch
the drips. The horses puff outside the door.

"Couple more minutes."

He dips and watches, dips and watches,
until the syrup slides off the scoop in one
smooth sheet.

"All right!" Gramp says. He opens a faucet on the side of the pan. Thick brown syrup pours into a kettle. At the other end of the pan, clear new sap flows in to replace it. Gramp shuts off the faucet. He puts some syrup in a glass and sets it in the snow to cool.

Nora can hardly wait to taste it. Maple syrup is even more special than sap. When the syrup is cool enough, Gramp and Nora drink some. It's so sweet they can only take little sips.

"Oh, that's good!" Gramp says.

Bonnie and Stella watch through the door.
"Bonnie and Stella should get a taste," Nora
says. "They brought the sap in, and they
brought the wood."

She pours some syrup into her hand. It's
warm and sticky, and it dribbles through her
fingers. Nora holds her hand out to Bonnie.

"Careful!" Gramp says.

Bonnie licks and licks. She thinks maple
syrup is special too.

Suddenly Nora feels Bonnie's teeth. "Ow!"
She pulls her hand away.

"Okay?" Gramp asks. Nora nods. "Your hand
was so sweet, she thought it was candy."

Stella points her ears. She wants syrup too, but Nora is afraid to give her any.

"Tell you what," Gramp says. "Take this kettle of syrup to Gram and tell her we want something we can give a horse. She'll know what you mean."

Gram puts the syrup on the stove, but she won't tell Nora what she's making.

"It'll be a surprise for you and the horses," she says.

So Nora takes supper down to Gramp, and they keep on boiling, long past Nora's bedtime.

When they come back, the kettle of syrup is gone, and the kitchen smells sweet and mapley.

Next morning after breakfast Gram brings
a brownie pan from the pantry. "Don't
look yet!" She cuts something into squares.
Then she gives a square to Nora.

"Maple sugar!" Nora says.

"We don't make it often," Gram says.
"Maple sugar's special."

"But so are horses!" says Nora. She bites
off a piece, and it tastes so good, it makes
the back corners of her mouth water. She
takes two more squares from the pan.

"Take one for Gramp, too," Gram says.

Bonnie and Stella are hitched to the sled.
They point their ears at Nora.
Nora holds her hands flat so her fingers are
out of the way.
Bonnie's and Stella's whiskers tickle, and
their breath goes *whoosh*. Their long lips
fumble up the sugar. *Crunch. Crunch. Crunch.*
They nod their heads as they chew.

"Happy now?" Gramp says.

"Yes," says Nora. She climbs up beside him.
Gramp gives her the reins, and she gives
him his piece of maple sugar.
Then they drive out to the woods to get
more sap.